For Deborah, Isobel, and Tom—D. B.

For Kippy, Ollie, and Jess.
I love the way you love me.—A. J.

SIMON & SCHUSTER BOOKS FOR YOUNG READERS
An imprint of Simon & Schuster Children's Publishing Division
1230 Avenue of the Americas, New York, New York 10020
Text copyright © 2004 by David Bedford
Illustrations copyright © 2004 by Ann James
First published in Australia in 2004 by Little Hare Books
First U.S. edition, 2005
SIMON & SCHUSTER BOOKS FOR YOUNG READERS is a trademark
of Simon & Schuster, Inc.
The text for this book is set in Garamond.
The illustrations are rendered in charcoal and watercolor.
Manufactured in China
10 9 8 7 6 5 4 3 2 1
CIP data for this book is available from the Library of Congress.
0-689-87625-4

THE WAY I LOVE YOU

DAVID BEDFORD & ANN JAMES

SIMON & SCHUSTER BOOKS FOR YOUNG READERS
NEW YORK   LONDON   TORONTO   SYDNEY

I love . . .

the way we play our games,

the way you run so fast,

the way you
come straight
back.

That's the way I love you.

I love . . .

the way we
always share,

the way you're
my best friend,

the way we
both pretend.

That's the way I love you.

I love . . .

the way you tell me things,

the way you
jump so high,

the way you
smile your
smile.

That's the way I love you.

I love . . .

the way you
understand,

the way you show me how,

the way we are
right now.

That's the way I love you.

I love . . .

the way you always care,

the way you're always there.

That's the way I love you.

That's the way I love you.